W9-BFE-786

Little Lies, Big Lies

A Book About Telling the Truth

By Barbara Shook Hazen
Illustrated by Cathy Beylon

Prepared with the cooperation of Bernice Berk, Ph.D., of the Bank Street College of Education

A GOLDEN BOOK · NEW YORK
Western Publishing Company, Inc., Racine, Wisconsin 53404

 Library of Congress Catalog Card Number: 86-80127.
ISBN 0-307-23288-3/ISBN 0-307-63288-1 (lib. bdg.) A B C D E F G H I J

Note to Parents

Lying is a common occurrence among young children. "Lies" may be intentional, such as when children express their wishes as fact. Or they may "lie" to protect themselves from things they are afraid of, such as punishment. Statements that we sometimes view as "lies" may actually tell parents a lot about their children's fears and hopes. Other "lies" are quite unintentional and come from the confusions inherent in a young child's incomplete understanding of the complex world. Distinguishing what is real and what is not, and what is "true" and what is not, can often be difficult for a young child—especially when he or she is upset.

Why do older children lie? Sometimes it's for a simple reason: They aren't encouraged to tell the truth. If children think that their parents only want to hear good things, they may feel they have to lie to be accepted and valued by an overly demanding or overly critical parent. Or children may lie to overcome feelings of inadequacy or to raise others' esteem for them.

Parents can foster honesty in children in a variety of ways. It won't be helpful to set traps or create situations in which a child may be inclined to lie. If you know a child has done something wrong, a good approach is to confront him or her, without shaming or humiliating the child or creating a climate of fear. Instead, encourage the child to express his or her feelings openly and really try to understand what the child is telling you.

An important way to discourage lying would be to practice and advocate the value of honesty yourself. Encouraging a child to be truthful helps build that bond of trust between parent and child on which love depends. It's also valuable for a child to learn the importance of being viewed as a trustworthy person by friends and other adults. Children can't always do this on their own. Your loving but firm guidance will help them develop a vital sense of integrity.

—The Editors

Aunt Una from Utah gave Scott a purple alligator sweater when she visited. She made it herself.

She didn't have any kids of her own and didn't know Scott very well, so she asked him how he liked it.

"Now, tell me the truth," she said cheerfully. "And tell me what you like."

Scott did. "The truth is, I'm very glad you thought of me," said Scott. "But I don't like purple alligators very much. What I really like are games, and sports stuff."

Scott's mother was horrified. "Now you've hurt Aunt Una's feelings," she chided.

"No, he hasn't," said Aunt Una. "Now I know what Scott really likes."

To Scott, Aunt Una said, "I'm glad you told me the truth. It makes me feel closer to you."

"Me, too," said Scott enthusiastically.

Sometimes, even in little things, it was hard to tell the truth. But not telling the truth had a way of backfiring.

That night, Scott lay in bed and remembered when he was a little kid, and he told Gram he loved the lima-bean casserole she spent all afternoon making.

He really didn't, but he didn't want to hurt her feelings.

After that, he had lima-bean casserole until it came out of his ears.

And it upset Gram that Scott didn't eat it—more than if he'd told the truth.

The next morning, Scott was still thinking about lies—all the different kinds, from small and harmless to HUGE AND HORRIBLE.

Small and harmless were the fish stories Grandpop told. When he talked about the fish he caught, it was "t-h-a-t big."

In photographs, it was "this big." Grandpop always winked when he told Scott, "A little exaggeration never hurts—as long as everybody knows."

And everybody knew Grandpop's fish stories were real whoppers.

Small and harmless was Scott's little brother, Craig, going around growling and saying he was a bear, and that he didn't have to drink his milk because bears don't drink milk.

Everybody knew Craig wasn't really a bear—even Craig.

Everyone said Craig had a very active imagination. He liked to make things up, which wasn't the same as lying.

Then there were excuse lies. They weren't so harmless, even if you got away with them.

When Scott got big enough to brush his teeth himself, his mother would ask, "Did you brush your teeth?"

Scott would say he had, even when he hadn't. And he showed her his toothbrush, which he wet with running water.

Now Scott really brushed his teeth—because he'd had a lot of cavities from not brushing when he was younger.

He got away with lying, but hurt himself in the long run.

He didn't get away with lying when he told his teacher, Miss Marcus, that a ferocious dog attacked him on the way to school and took off with his math homework, which was why he didn't have it to hand in.

Miss Marcus made Scott stay after school and do two sets of math problems—because he'd lied, and because he wouldn't learn math if he didn't do the problems.

"Telling the truth is a matter of responsibility," Miss Marcus said. "It's for your own good."

But sometimes, it was hard to tell the truth.

When Scott's father asked him, "What happened to the watch I gave you?" Scott gulped, and told him the truth.

"Somebody took it out of my locker," Scott said.

"And was it locked?" Scott's father asked.

"I, uh, forgot to lock it," Scott admitted.

Scott thought his father would get mad at him for being careless. Instead, he was very understanding. "I know that hurts," he said. He also said he'd go halves on helping Scott get a new one. And in the future, he told Scott to lock up, because not everyone was honest.

Scott knew his mother would get mad when he broke the china bowl in the living room.

It was his mother's favorite, and he wasn't supposed to be playing basketball in the living room in the first place.

Scott lied when his mother asked, "Do you know where my bowl is?"

He shook his head and said, "No, I don't."

It was a big lie. But Scott made it even bigger by hiding the pieces in one of his puzzle boxes.

He worried every time someone came into his room. He felt jumpy and awful.

Then Scott did something that made the lie HUGE AND HORRIBLE.

It happened one day when Scott was mad at Craig. Craig got to go outside and play with their mother, while Scott had to stay inside and finish his homework.

What Scott did was put the broken pieces in Craig's room—under the comforter, where his mother was sure to find them.

She did, and was furious at Craig, who said, "But I didn't do it."

At first, Scott felt like he'd gotten away with something, and gotten even with Craig.

But the smug feeling didn't last. Craig started to cry. He cried all through dinner, and didn't stop.

Even worse, their mother said, "Accidents happen. I don't mind your breaking the bowl half as much as I mind your lying to me and hiding the pieces."

Then she said, "No dessert, and no TV for two weeks."

Craig cried harder. Scott felt guilty and miserable. But he was even more afraid that everyone would be furious with him if they knew what *really* happened.

It got worse. That night, Scott's stomach hurt. It wasn't from dinner. His worries about the lie were gnawing at him.

When his mother tucked him in, she said, "Scott, you're acting funny. Is there something you want to tell me?"

"No," said Scott, which was another lie.

That was one of the worst things about big lies. You had to keep lying, to save your own skin and to keep from being found out.

That night, Scott couldn't sleep. He was afraid of being punished. Even worse, he was afraid his mother wouldn't love him if he told her the awful thing he did. And his father would call him bad. And they both might send him away.

The next morning, Scott couldn't stand the way he felt. He went to his parents' room.

"I have something to tell you," he said.

He stood in the doorway and told them everything.

Then he said, "I didn't mean to be so bad," and started crying.

"What you did was wrong," Scott's father said in his serious voice. "Very wrong. It was the worst kind of lie because it hurt someone else, someone who trusted you. But Craig has told lies, too, and with time, you can get back his trust."

His mother said nothing.

"Are you going to send me away?"

"Never, because we both love you, no matter what you do," his mother said. "But no TV and no desserts for a month. I also want you to apologize to Craig—and think about the trouble your lie caused."

"I can't stop thinking about it," Scott said as his mother and father both circled him in a hug.

After that, Scott tried to tell the truth. He knew how lies bounced back and hit the liar.

He told the truth about sneaking a peek at the Christmas presents in the closet when Craig was about to be blamed.

He said he opened the closet by accident, but then couldn't resist taking a look.

His mother got very angry and Scott got punished, but Craig said, "Thanks," and gave him a chocolate-covered raisin.

Scott also told the truth to grouchy-looking Mr. Smudge next door — that it was his baseball that broke his window.

"Harrumph!" said Mr. Smudge. "Mighty long hit. And I won't make you pay for it, because you 'fessed up."

That made Scott happy. Afterwards, he always waved to Mr. Smudge, who always smiled at Scott and waved back.

The next time Aunt Una visited she gave Scott a new baseball glove, and a ski sweater she'd knitted.

"How do you like them?" Aunt Una asked as Scott tried on both his presents.

"Just what I wanted," said Scott.

Aunt Una hugged Scott and said, "I wouldn't have known if you hadn't told me. And that's the truth!"